Remember Me When...

Illustrated by Ciara Compton

ChalicePress.com

Print: 9780827233140

Printed in the United States of America

Remember Me When...

Creating Memories to Last a Lifetime

Written by Todd Williams
Illustrated by Ciara Compton

The grandfather sat with his grandchild one day and said,

"You know I love you very much, and I will always be with you.

"When my body stops working and God brings me home to heaven, you and I can still be with each other in different ways.

"You can..."

Remember me when
        you see butterflies
                flutter in the sky.

Remember me when
you laugh out loud.

you play in the mud.

Remember me when
you blow bubbles.

Remember me when

you twirl in your dress.

you watch fireflies light up
the summer sky.

Remember me when...

you throw paper airplanes.

you eat strawberries in the spring.

Remember me when
    you build sandcastles on the beach.

Remember me when
    you dip cookies in milk.

you play dress-up.

Remember me when...

you see lanterns fly into the sky.

Remember me when...

Use this space to create the ways you want to be remembered.